The Football Shirt

Written by Catherine MacPhail

Illustrated by Paul Fisher

 Collins

Chapter 1

Ross first saw the football shirt that Wednesday morning. It was pinned on to the tree by the roadside. There was a football scarf wound round one of the branches and flowers had been laid at the bottom of the tree. There were cards there too. Someone had died here. Ross had heard about the accident. A boy, Thomas Tully, had lost control of his motorbike and crashed into this tree. Thomas Tully. Ross remembered seeing his photograph in the paper, a smiling boy with a mop of bright red hair. He had still been a teenager, the report said, a boy with a great career in football ahead of him. It had all been snatched away the day his motorbike had crashed into this tree.

LOCAL BOY
DIES IN CRASH

Local boy, Thomas Tully, was killed today when his motorbike hit a tree on the

Ross couldn't take his eyes off that football shirt. It was the very latest top of his favourite team, the best team in the world. It was a really special top, a limited edition. There'd only been a few made. Ross was saving up for that very football shirt himself. And here it was, pinned to a tree.

It was such a waste. That football shirt was made to be worn. Worn by a boy like him. A boy like Ross.

Ross gasped. What was he thinking? He drew his eyes away from the tree, got back on his bike and pedalled home.

The first thing he did when he got home was to take his tin from under his bed and count his money. He'd never have enough money for that football shirt. It had taken him ages to save this much. He should just ask his mum or dad for the money, but of course he couldn't do that. Money was tight at the moment. Mum only worked part time, and Dad wasn't even sure if he'd have a job for much longer. No, he couldn't ask them for the money. He'd just have to keep saving.

But that night, as he lay in bed, he dreamt of the football shirt. He dreamt of it pinned to that tree, wishing it was anywhere else but there. He woke up and heard the rain battering against his window, and he thought about the shirt again. He thought about it as if it was almost human, cold and wet, wishing it was warm and dry. He felt sorry  for it. It didn't want to be there stuck to that tree.

The next day on his way to school, he passed the tree again, and there was the shirt, soaking wet, glistening in the early morning sun. It seemed to shine so brightly against the dark trunk of the tree.

It's a waste, a voice whispered to him. *It shouldn't be there. Tully's dead. He doesn't need or want the shirt any longer, does he?*

Ross dragged himself away from the tree. He went to school, but he didn't listen in any of the lessons, he hardly talked to any of his friends. All he thought about that day was the football shirt. He couldn't get it out of his mind.

Chapter 2

Ross stopped again at the tree on his way home and stared at the shirt.

"I'm surprised it's still there," his friend, Tony said. Ross jumped when he heard his voice. He was so caught up in his own world, he hadn't heard him coming.

"What's still there?" he asked, but he knew what Tony was talking about.

Tony pointed to the tree, "That football shirt. That's the one you're saving so hard for, isn't it? And there it is, stuck to a tree, doing nobody any good. It's a wonder nobody's stolen it already."

"That would be a terrible thing to do," Ross said.

Tony only shrugged his shoulders. "You can't steal from a dead boy, can you?"

You can't steal from a dead boy. The words repeated and repeated themselves in Ross's head. Over and over, louder and louder. He went home and counted his money again. Not enough. He'd never have enough.

Tony was right. It was a waste to have that shirt stuck to the tree, doing nobody any good.

Who'd know if he took it, he told himself? Who'd ever find out? Who'd care?

When darkness fell, he knew what he was going to do.

He was going to steal that shirt.

Chapter 3

Ross had never left the house this late before. He'd never gone out without his parents knowing. He waited until well after dinner, when his mum was in the bath, his dad was snoozing on the sofa and his little sister was safely tucked up in her cot. He wouldn't be gone for long. They'd never miss him. It was a pitch black night. The moon was hidden behind the clouds. The streets were quiet and empty.
He almost felt like a criminal, cycling through the town, keeping close to the walls so no one could see him.

At last he reached the tree. The football shirt seemed to glow in the darkness. It was almost as if, and he knew this was crazy, but it was almost as if the shirt was speaking to him. As if it was saying, *I knew you'd come. Take me home.*

He looked from left to right, but there was no one about. The street was silent. His hands shook as he took the pins from the shirt, one by one, from each of the shoulders and from one side and then the other. The football shirt seemed to fall into his hands, as if it belonged there.

You can't steal from a dead boy. He heard the words again in his head, so clearly, it was almost as if someone close by had spoken them.

But he was alone. Just Ross, and the football shirt.

He stuffed it under his jacket, and cycled home. A police car came into view and Ross darted into a side street. For a moment he was sure they were coming for him. They knew what he'd done.

That was silly, of course. How could they know? And anyway ... you can't steal from a dead boy. That's not a crime, is it?

He had to be very quiet coming into the house, but he already had his story if his mum or dad did find him suddenly sneaking in the back door. He'd say he had only popped out to make sure he'd locked his bike up safely. But no one saw him. His mum heard him in the kitchen and she called out, "Homework finished, Ross?" She thought he'd been in his bedroom all this time.

"Yes Mum," he called back, and then he tiptoed upstairs and went into the bathroom. He pulled the shirt from under his jacket.

It was wet and dirty, but it looked as good as ever to him. He turned on the taps and dipped the shirt into the hot, soapy water. Once it was clean, it would be as good as new.

Ross slept so well that night. The last thing he saw was the shirt hanging on the wardrobe door. It was going to be too big for him, of course – Tully had been a lot older than Ross – but who cared about that? He'd grow into it. All he could think of was that the shirt was his now. It belonged to him.

The shirt was the first thing he saw when he woke up. It was dry now, and it looked brilliant. Any guilt he'd felt the night before was gone. He'd done the right thing.

This shirt was meant to be worn. He'd give the money he'd already saved to charity ... in fact, he'd find out what Tully's favourite charity was, and he'd give the money to that one. Yes, he could make up for taking the shirt that way.

But there was no doubt in his head. This shirt was meant to be worn and he'd done the right thing.

Chapter 4

It was all the talk when he got to school that day. Tully's football shirt had been taken from the tree. There'd even been an item on the local radio about it that morning.

"Who'd do such a terrible thing?" Lily wanted to know. Lily was in his class.

Tony broke in, "I don't think it was so terrible. It was wasted stuck on that tree. I'm surprised it stayed there as long as it did."

"Trust you, Tony," Lily said. "Someone pinned that shirt up there out of respect. Whoever stole it should be ashamed of themselves."

When Lily saw him wearing the shirt, she'd know Ross had been the one who took it. Lily was too smart. Ross decided he'd better say something, "My mum's off to get me my shirt today."

"Did you save up the money, Ross? Good for you," Tony said, slapping him on the back.

Lily looked at him. "You told us last week you'd never have enough money to buy it."

"Well, I did have enough. OK?"

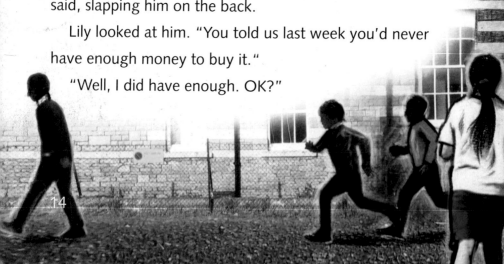

Lily sucked in her cheeks. She tapped her teeth with her finger. "Let me see ... you suddenly have enough money for the football shirt ... and the shirt on the tree goes missing? Mmm, now that's funny, isn't it?"

"Don't listen to her, Ross," Tony said. "She thinks she's a detective. Sherlock Lily."

He pulled Ross away, but Lily kept on watching him. As if she knew. He couldn't help thinking she knew. What she said bothered him. Who else would think that he'd stolen the shirt?

He wore it for the first time in public, on Saturday. He was going into town with his mates. He felt so good when he put it on. It must have shrunk when he'd washed it, because now it fitted him perfectly, as if it was made for him.

And now, no one would believe it was Tully's shirt. Tully's shirt would never have fitted him so well.

Lily, however, was still suspicious. He met her in the café. She came up to him and began inspecting the shirt. "It looks exactly like the one that was on the tree," she said.

Ross sighed. "It's a football shirt, Lily, they all look the same."

"Do they?" She came closer and whispered, "So why has yours got pin marks at the shoulders, as if it has been pinned up somewhere ... like ... on a tree?"

Ross felt his face go red. He'd forgotten the pin marks. "Oh listen to Sherlock Lily here. Knows everything." He was thinking fast. He licked his lips. "If you must know, that was how I was able to afford it. They gave me it cheap because it had been pinned up in the window."

Now it was Lily's turn to blush. She stepped back. "Oh," was all she said, and she moved off with her friends.

How had he ever learnt to lie like that? Ross was a boy who never lied, yet somehow that lie had come so easily.

He could do it because he was meant to have this shirt, he told himself. That's why he could lie so well. No doubt about it. That was the answer. He felt good wearing the shirt. Everyone said how much it suited him. How good he looked in it. He'd done the right thing ... and now, with that little lie, no one would ever find out the truth.

Chapter 5

His mum was there when he got home. Ross had planned to
rush upstairs and take the shirt off before she saw it.
Her eyes went wide when she saw him wearing it.

"When did you get that? I didn't know you'd saved
enough money to buy it."

Ross took a deep breath. "I ... I got a bargain.
This one was pinned up in the window. Look," he held
out the shoulders so she could inspect the pin marks.
"The lady in the shop let me have it cheap."

He'd never lied to his mother, yet he didn't even blush.

She patted him on the back. "Clever boy. Always look for a bargain; that's what I do too." She smiled at him. She was proud of him. Would she be as proud if she knew the truth, Ross wondered?

He ran up to his room and slammed the door shut. He'd told his mum a lie. Yet, when he saw himself in the mirror, all his guilt left him. He looked great in it. He loved this football shirt.

The next day was Sunday, and on Sundays he played
football with his friends at the park. Not very well, he had
to admit. But somehow, now that he had the football shirt,
he'd a feeling that it might just make a difference to the way
he played. Thomas Tully had had a great future ahead of
him as a football player. Everyone said so. Now that he was
wearing the shirt, Ross thought maybe he could be a great
football player too.

He walked to the park with a
spring in his step. Today, he was
going to be the best.

"You look different today, Ross,"
Tony said when he walked on to
the pitch.

"I feel different," Ross agreed.
He could see Lily and her friends
watching them from the sidelines.
Something about the way she
stared at him made his face go red.
He turned his back on her.

"Let's get on with the game,"
he shouted.

They began to play. The ball was coming his way.
Ross could have a great shot from here. He leapt for the ball.

He was going to head it straight into the goal. He missed and landed with a splat in the mud.

"What happened there, Ross?" Tony came up to him and helped him to his feet. Ross was embarrassed. What *had* happened there? How could he have missed the ball when it had been so close?

"I'm fine," he told Tony. He was still sure the shirt would bring him luck.

The game went on. Ross missed kick after kick.
He'd never played so badly.

It was almost the end of the first half and his team were
awarded a free kick. Ross insisted on taking it. "I feel lucky,"
he said.

"You haven't been very lucky up till now,"
Tony reminded him.

Everyone held their breath. Ross ran for the ball.
He kicked it high into the air. And then he slipped on
the mud and fell flat on his back again. It didn't matter.
He'd scored a great goal.

"What happened this time?" Tony yelled.

"It must have been a goal!" Ross shouted. Everyone was yelling at him. Lily and her friends were all laughing as if he had done something funny.

He got to his feet, and there, on the pitch in front of him, was the football. It hadn't moved. "But I kicked it. I felt it. I saw it, it was headed for the goal." He'd felt the touch of it when his foot made contact. So why was the ball still sitting there on the ground?

"You missed it by a mile," Tony said. He slapped him on the back. "It's just not your day."

And it wasn't. In the second half, no matter how he tried, he couldn't do anything right. When the ball came his way, he missed it. When he was running after the ball he slipped in the mud. The only time he did score a goal, it was for the other side.

Ross was never so glad to hear the full-time whistle. The shirt hadn't made him a better player at all. In fact, he was a hundred times worse than he'd ever been.

He looked over at Lily. She was smirking at him. She looked so pleased he'd made a fool of himself. But Ross didn't look at Lily for long. It was the boy standing behind her who caught his eye.

Bright red hair, blue eyes, Ross had seen his photo in the papers. Thomas Tully ... and he was staring right at him. Ross gasped. He began to shake. Tully was saying something to him, and though he was so far away, Ross was sure he could hear every word: "Put it back."

Chapter 6

Ross grabbed at Tony's shirt. "Look there, do you see that?"

Tony followed Ross's pointed finger. "It's only Lily and her friends. Let them laugh."

"No. I mean him!" But when Ross looked again, there was no one there. Tully was gone.

"Who?" Tony peered closer. "Oh you mean Zak Brown? What about him?"

Zak Brown, one of the older pupils in the school, looked across at them and waved. Zak Brown, he had red hair too, just like Tully, but Zak's was not quite so bright.

And it was Tully he'd seen a moment ago … wasn't it?

Ross almost told Tony, "I saw Thomas Tully. He was standing there in the crowd." But it sounded crazy. It was impossible. Wasn't it? It must have been all in his imagination.

He couldn't have seen Thomas Tully. Thomas Tully was dead.

Yet, the words he'd heard him say bothered him all that day.

Put it back.

They always went to the cinema on a Sunday after
the match; Lily and her friends came too. Ross began to
forget what he'd seen. He told himself it had all been
in his mind.

Until Tully appeared on the screen.

There he was, standing in a crowd, and it was as if he
saw Ross sitting there. He began to walk towards him.

Then he stopped. Tully's face filled the whole screen, and
he stared at Ross.

"Do you see him? You must see him!" Ross pulled
at Tony.

Tony looked from Ross to the screen. "See who?"

Then Tully spoke, "Put it back."

How did none of them hear those words? *Put it back*.

Ross got to his feet. He had to get out of here, get away from that screen. He stumbled along the row. He knocked Lily's popcorn all over her, and her drink spilled on the floor. He'd never been so clumsy.

"What's wrong with you?" Lily snapped.

"He feels sick," Tony said. "Leave him be."

But Ross didn't feel sick. He felt scared.

Tony followed him. Ross turned round to tell him
to go back. He'd be fine now. He was going home.

As he turned he felt something wrapping itself around
his ankle. He looked down, but there was nothing there.
It grew tighter. He could feel himself begin to fall. He reached
out for something to hold on to, but there was nothing.

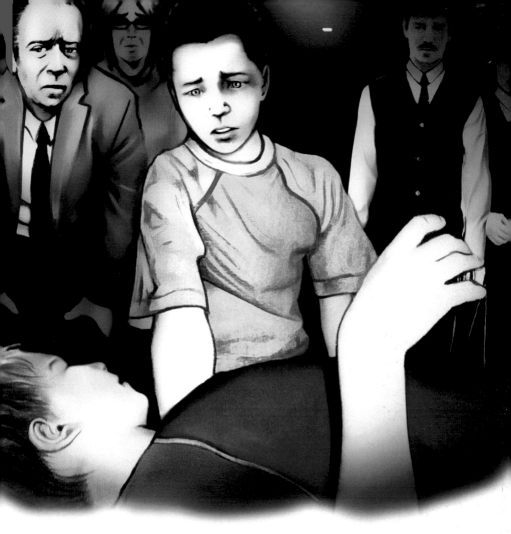

"Is anything broken?"

Ross opened his eyes and Tony was there in front of him.
He looked worried.

There were other people there too, bending over him.

"I'm fine," Ross told them.

"This just isn't your lucky day," Tony said.

Chapter 7

Ross woke up that night in a cold sweat. He didn't
feel well. He was coming down with a cold. That was it.
Nothing else.

The room was in darkness. Ross looked at the shirt
hanging on the wardrobe door, freshly washed. It was *his*
football shirt. His!

"Put it back."

Ross jumped when he heard the words, but they must
have been only in his head. He was alone in the room,
wasn't he? Or ... Ross peered over the covers, and turned
ice cold. Thomas Tully's face was staring back at him from
his mirror.

"Put it back," he was saying. "Put. It. Back."

Ross let out a yell. He reached for the table lamp and fumbled for the switch. He pulled the cable so hard the lamp fell to the ground. The light came on. Ross looked back at the mirror.

Thomas Tully was gone. It was only his own face he saw in the mirror. It was only his own reflection he saw, a boy with a scared face and his hair almost standing on end.

His dad burst into the room. "What happened, Ross?"
He looked at the lamp on the floor, at Ross's white face.
"Are you OK?"

Ross nodded. "I had a bad dream," he said. And that
wasn't a lie. It must have been a dream, just a bad dream.

His dad smiled. "Read something cheery for a while
before you go back to sleep. Remember, we're only in
the next room."

His dad left the door open a little and Ross was glad
of that. Even though it had only been a dream. It had been
his own reflection he had seen in the mirror. It hadn't been
Thomas Tully. As if Thomas Tully could appear in his mirror!

As if he could appear on a cinema screen! And the words, those words ... *put it back* ... that had all been in his mind too.

He kept the light on all night, and didn't close his eyes once. He stared at the mirror, then looked back to the shirt hanging on the wardrobe door.

And though he kept telling himself it had only been a bad dream, it had all been in his imagination, he couldn't stop those words pounding in his head. *Put it back.* Like a ticking clock. *Put it back. Put it back.*

Chapter 8

He fell asleep in class the next day. Mr Bell, the teacher, slammed a book down on his desk to wake him up and the class all laughed. Lily leaned across and whispered to him, "You look terrible. Not sleeping?"

"I had a bad dream," he muttered.

"I'm not surprised. Perhaps you're feeling guilty. That's why you can't sleep. What do you think?"

Ross snapped at her, "I didn't steal that shirt."

"I wish I could believe that," Lily said. He'd never convince Lily.

"I think you'd better wake yourself up, Ross," Mr Bell said. "Go to the toilets, splash some water on your face."

Ross was glad to get out of the classroom. It was too stuffy, and he was beginning to feel sick. Perhaps he did have some kind of a bug. He even thought about just going home. Then he remembered his room and the mirror and knew he'd rather be in school.

Ross could hear teachers shouting somewhere on another corridor. Pupils were all at lessons, so the toilets were empty.

Ross turned on the tap. He bent his head, closed his eyes, and cupped his hands full of the cold water, and splashed it against his face. It felt good. He did it again. Then he stood straight and opened his eyes.

And Thomas Tully was there in the mirror, his ice blue eyes boring into him. Ross couldn't breathe. He tried to yell, but he couldn't make a sound. Thomas Tully was there in the mirror, but when Ross swung round ... he wasn't. There was no one else in the toilet but himself. Yet when he looked back again to the mirror there was Thomas Tully, staring back at him.

"Put it back," he was saying.

Ross covered his face with his hands. "Go away! Go away!" he shouted. He wanted him gone.

It seemed ages before he pulled his hands from his face. Thomas Tully was no longer there. It was just his own tired, scared reflection looking back at him. Ross let out a sigh of relief, but his sigh turned to a silent scream. Words began to form on the mirror, and he knew at once what those words would be. Each letter appeared as if an invisible hand was writing them.

Ross couldn't take any more. He ran from the toilets and
bumped right into Tony.

"Mr Bell sent me to look for you." Tony said. "Are you
feeling OK? You look terrible."

Ross grabbed him by the shoulders. "In the toilets ...
there's something written on the mirror ... look ...
you'll see." He pushed Tony in front of him. He wanted him
to see those words too. Ross stood at the door with his
eyes closed. He was too afraid to look.

"There's nothing written on the mirror, Ross," Tony said. Ross opened his eyes and stepped inside the toilets and it was true. The words had gone from the mirror, and that seemed scarier than anything else.

"But, it was there, it was definitely there … I saw it …"

"What did it say?" Tony asked.

Ross said nothing. He knew then he couldn't tell Tony the words he'd seen. Because then he'd have to tell him what the words meant. Tell him that he was the one who'd stolen the football shirt.

"Maybe I didn't see anything. It was my imagination. I don't feel well," he said at last.

"I think you should go home," Tony told him. "You've got a bug or something. I'll tell the teacher."

Ross was quick to agree. He wanted to go home. His mum would be there. He wouldn't be alone.

Chapter 9

He cycled all the way home, jumped from his bike at his door and took out his front door key. It was only then he knew something strange was happening. The wind blew through the trees. The sun dipped behind the clouds. The street was empty. No one was about. Ross turned his head slowly and looked up to the end of the street. There he was again. Thomas Tully.

He just stood there, watching him. Ross began to shake. He fumbled with his key.

Tully began to walk towards him. Step by step, he was coming closer with each second. Yet the street was still silent. There was no sound of his footsteps on the pavement.

Ross couldn't get the key in the lock. His hand was shaking so much the key fell to the ground.

He tried to pick it up. It was as if his fingers had turned to claws. He couldn't make them open to grip the key. And Thomas Tully still came closer. At last the key was in his hand. He tried again to get it into the lock. He kept looking up at Tully, moving closer. Soon he would be close enough to touch him. "Get away from me!" he shouted. Tully only shook his head and moved closer.

"Put it back," Tully said. His voice seemed to come from down a long tunnel. It sounded like the echo of a voice. "Put it back."

Still he came closer. If he reached out now, he could touch Ross, grip him by the shoulders, drag him ... where? Ross didn't want to think about where he would drag him. No!

At last, the key slid into the lock. Ross opened his door. Tully was almost at his elbow when he threw himself inside and slammed the door shut.

Ross backed against the wall. At any moment he expected the ghost of Tully to seep through the door like smoke. Nothing came, but still he heard the words so clearly. *Put it back.*

He'd taken enough. He leant exhausted against the door, and whispered, "I will. I promise. I'll put it back. Just let me be."

He sat in his bedroom until it was dark, clutching the shirt to his chest. He had to wait until it was dark before he could leave. Ross hoped Tully would realise that.
He couldn't pin it back on the tree in broad daylight. In his room all that day he kept whispering the words, hoping Tully could hear him. "I'm putting it back. I'm putting it back."

It had been the wrong thing to do, stealing the shirt. Ross knew that now. He couldn't understand what had made him do it in the first place. He was not that kind of boy. He'd never been that kind of boy. The shirt had brought him nothing but bad luck. Ross sat on his bed and longed for night time.

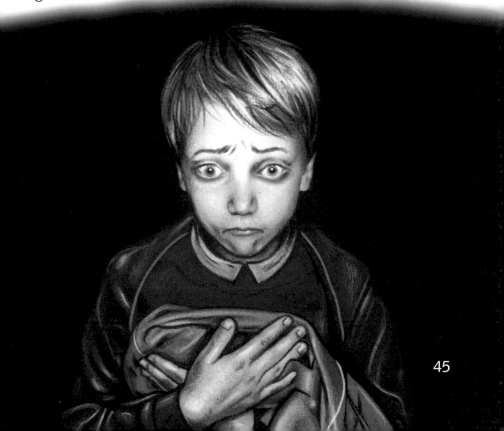

45

The house was silent when he began to leave. His mum
was at her keep-fit class, his little sister was sleeping and his
dad was reading the paper in the living room. Ross took
the shirt and stuffed it inside his rucksack. He even
remembered the pins he needed to attach it to the tree again.

He took his bike and cycled to the tree. The street
was quiet. There were hardly any houses here.

He shook as he pinned the top back on to the tree. It kept
falling over his hands, as if it didn't want to leave him, and
for a split second he almost changed his mind.
It was his shirt now. It belonged to him.

But then he remembered Thomas Tully, and he knew he
couldn't go through that again. He'd made a promise
to Tully. He wouldn't break it now. Once he'd put the shirt
back, Tully would leave him alone.

47

At last it was done. The shirt was back where it belonged, there on the tree. And as soon as he'd done it, Ross knew it had been the right thing to do.

He slept like a log that night. He hardly stirred. He'd no fear now of Tully suddenly appearing. No terror of seeing those words on a mirror. In fact, Ross had no dreams at all.

He woke up the next morning, and took a long stretch on his bed. It was going to be a good day.

He leapt out of bed and opened his wardrobe door and his spine turned to ice.

The football shirt was back.

Chapter 10

This couldn't be happening. Ross had put it back on the tree last night, hadn't he? But here it was hanging in his wardrobe.

Ross shook his head. "No! Tully, I put it back, I swear. I put it back!" He was so afraid Tully would appear again, here in the room. He looked all around, but there was no one, nothing he could see.

He must have dreamt he'd put it back. That was it. It had all been a dream. He'd slept so soundly last night, and he'd only dreamt he had made that journey on his bike back to the tree. Pinning it up had been part of that dream too. It hadn't really happened. Of course that was the explanation.

It hadn't really happened.

He looked all around the room again, just in case Tully was watching him to see what he'd do. "Tonight, Tully, I promise I'll put it back tonight."

And he did.

Once more, he waited until it was dark. He took his bike and pedalled madly along the empty streets towards that tree.

It looked stark against the night sky. Its leaves quivered
in the breeze. The flowers that had been laid there were
faded now. The football scarf was still wound round
a branch. No one had tried to steal that.

Ross stepped forward. He held the shirt in front of him. "This is not a dream," he whispered. "This is really happening."

He took great care pinning the shirt on the tree. He sank one pin after another deep into the trunk. It was done at last. As he pulled his hand away a splinter bit into his finger. He let out a yell of pain, then looked around in case anyone had heard him. The street was still empty. Ross stood for a moment just looking at the football shirt. It was there. He told himself, it was definitely there. No dream this time.

He lay in bed that night determined not to go to sleep. He'd make sure it didn't come back. But his eyes kept closing and finally he drifted into an uneasy sleep.

The shirt was the first thing he thought about when he woke up. He jumped to his feet and threw open the wardrobe door, and almost yelled out with fright.

It was back again!

It couldn't be. It couldn't have been another dream? This wasn't happening. He clenched his fist and drew in his breath with the pain. He looked at his hand. It still had the splinter in it. The splinter he'd got last night when he pinned the shirt on the tree.

It hadn't been a dream. Yet, how had the shirt managed to come back? It was impossible.

But it was impossible to see a dead person too, wasn't it?

Ross was afraid. He didn't know what to do. He wanted to be rid of that shirt so much. He suddenly hated it. He snatched it from the hanger and ran downstairs. He threw it in the rubbish. The bin men were coming today, they'd take it. Let them. He wanted it gone.

He fell asleep in class again.

Mr Bell asked him if there was anything wrong, "Or were you up late watching television?"

"Sorry Sir," Ross said. When Mr Bell suggested he go to the toilets to splash his face, he told him no, "I'll be fine, Sir." He didn't dare go back there. Tully might be waiting for him.

Lily was still watching him. *She knows,* Ross thought, *she's known all along.*

Even Tony knew something was wrong. "You can tell me," he said. "I'm your best friend."

But Ross couldn't tell anyone.

He trudged back from school and went straight up to his bedroom as soon as he was home. He bit into his knuckles to stop from screaming.

The shirt was back. It was hanging once again on his wardrobe door. He felt as if it was talking to him. It was saying, *You'll never get rid of me.*

Ross snatched it from the hanger again and ran downstairs. His mum was in the living room. "You almost lost that," she said as soon as she saw the shirt in his hand. "You must have put it in the rubbish by mistake. I got it out just in time or the bin men would have been off with it."

She smiled at him, as if she'd done him a big favour. Ross wanted to tell her everything, but how could he? He'd have to admit he'd stolen the shirt in the first place, and the rest ...? It all sounded unbelievable. All he could say was, "Thanks Mum."

His bedroom was cold when he went back in there. Too cold, and Ross knew at once that Tully was there somewhere.

It was his voice he heard first, "Put it back."

Then Tully stepped from the shadows in the corner of his room. "Put it back." He spoke so softly it was almost a whisper.

Ross jumped backwards toward the wardrobe, terrified of what Tully would do. "I'm trying. I'm trying," he said. "Can't you see I'm trying?"

When he looked again, Tully was gone. It was as if he'd melted into the shadows.

Ross had to do something. He had to put the shirt back. But how?

Chapter 11

Ross found himself back at the tree. He'd wandered out of the house after his dinner and didn't really know where he was going. It was as if his feet just led him here. He stood staring at it.

There was a boy there laying fresh flowers. He turned when he saw Ross. "Did you know him?" he asked. "Tully, I mean?"

Ross shook his head. "No ..." he said. *But I know him now,* he was thinking, *now that he's dead.*

"He was my best friend," the boy said.

"I'm sorry," said Ross. "It was a terrible accident."

The boy nodded towards the tree, "See someone stole the shirt."

Ross felt his face go red. His voice shook, "That was terrible too."

"Was it? I don't know if it was. I'm glad it's gone," the boy said.

Ross looked at him. Had he heard him right? "What do you mean?"

"From the day he got it, that shirt brought him nothing but bad luck."

Ross felt a cold shiver go down his spine. He had to know more. "How do you mean ... bad luck ...?"

"I remember the day he got it," the boy went on. It was as if he needed to tell someone. "We'd just played the final in the youth league. Tully had scored the winning goal. He was man of the match. The coach was so pleased, he told him he was going to give him a present, a special present.

He went off and came back with this wooden box. He had to open it with a key, and the football shirt was inside.

The coach said it had been left in one of the lockers but no one had claimed it. He said it was a waste for such a terrific shirt to lie in a locked box ... so he presented it to Tully.

I mean, it's a limited edition. Everyone wants that shirt. And Tully was so proud of it. But that's when the bad things started to happen."

"What kind of things?" Ross asked.

The boy shrugged, "He was missing goals at games.
The ball would sail right over the bar, when you knew it
could have gone into the net. He was scoring own goals."
The boy shook his head. "He wasn't sleeping properly.
He said he was having nightmares, but I think there was
more to it. I think it was that shirt."

Ross could feel his heart pounding. "That shirt?"

"I know, it sounds stupid," the boy said, "but at the last match he ever played, a scout was there from one of the big teams. He'd come to see Tully. If he played well, the scout was going to sign him. And he never played as badly as he did that day – like a boy with two left feet. The scout didn't sign him. Tully was so upset ... he said it was the shirt. "

"It was the shirt's fault." The boy thought it was a question. He didn't know that Ross was agreeing with him. He knew Tully had been right. It *was* the shirt.

"Sounds even crazier now, but the day Tully died … he told me, he was putting the shirt back. That's what he kept saying … I'm putting it back. That's where he was going when he crashed his bike. He was going back to the football ground, to lock it back in that box. He just never made it."

Chapter 12

Ross knew now what he had to do. He knew at last what Tully really meant. He hadn't been trying to scare him. He'd been trying to warn him. *Put it back*. Warn him that there was something about that football shirt, something dangerous. Ross knew he had to get rid of it quickly.

Put it back. It was what Tully had been trying to do when he died. He'd been trying to put it back.

Now it was Ross who had to put it back. He was going to put it back into that box at the football ground, and he was going to lock it away forever.

He hurried home. The shirt was back on the hanger. Ross grabbed it and stuffed it in his rucksack. How had he ever been fooled by it? It was as if the shirt had cast a spell on him. Now the spell was broken.

"I'm putting it back," Ross whispered. He felt a chill in the room. And he said it louder, so Tully would hear. "I'm putting it back, Tully. I'm putting it back for you."

He took his bike and began to cycle to the other end of the town where the football ground was. Faster and faster he went. He pedalled as if his life depended on getting there and putting the shirt in that box. He swerved to avoid a van coming out of a side street.

"Watch where you're going you little so-and-so!" the driver leaned out of the cab and yelled at him.

But Ross didn't stop or slow down.

In fact, he cycled faster. Some force was making him ride even faster, as if there was no time to lose.

As he was coming to the top of the hill he hit the brakes.

They didn't work. They'd been working this morning, nothing wrong with them at all. Yet now, no matter how hard he pressed them, nothing happened. It'd be downhill all the way after this, downhill with no brakes on his bike.

It was the shirt. The shirt was trying to stop him getting there.

This was what had happened to Tully. Ross knew it now. Tully had tried to put the shirt back and the shirt had stopped him. He could almost see Tully struggling with his motorbike, not being able to stop, losing control, crashing into the tree. It had been the football shirt.

Well it wasn't going to stop him.

Ross had never felt so afraid. How could he stop
the bike? He was over the top of the hill now and going
down fast. At the bottom of the hill there was a junction
with traffic lights. If the lights were red, he'd never be able
to stop. He'd crash into the traffic coming the other way.

He yelled out. He was going so fast his feet couldn't stay
on the pedals. Down and down he went. He prayed for
the lights to turn green.

They turned green just as he reached them. Ross raced
through them, and aimed his bike on to the grass by the
side of the road. The bike toppled. Ross somersaulted over
the handlebars. He rolled over and over, but he wasn't
going to let anything stop him. He couldn't. He was on his
feet in an instant.

"Are you OK?" A man was running towards him.

Ross waved at him, "I'm fine. Honest." He was close enough now to run to the football ground. He grabbed his rucksack and left his bike on the grass.

"You're not going to win," he said softly. "We won't let you win."

Chapter 13

Ross had been to this football ground. A lot of the school matches were played here. The gates were open, a youth game was in progress, so Ross could get in easily. He hurried through the corridors towards the dressing room. There were shirts hanging on doors, football boots on seats, lockers lying open. Ross looked all around. What if, after all this, the box was gone? Perhaps someone had thrown it out. What if he couldn't find it? He hauled open lockers. He looked under benches. It had to be here. Finally, he saw it. The box was sitting on a window ledge, still lying open.

Ross jumped up on a bench. He pulled the box down. The key was still in the lock. He took a deep breath and pulled the shirt from his rucksack. It was as if it didn't want to go in. He felt it fight against him.

"You're going back!" he said, and he gripped it tightly and pushed it inside the box. Why, he wondered, would a football shirt like this be locked in a box? Unless ... unless someone else had discovered what this shirt could do. They'd locked it in this box and left it here, and hoped that was the end of it. That was why no one had ever claimed it.

Well, he wasn't going to make the same mistake.

At last it was in. Ross slammed down the lid and turned the key. He knew there was a cellar in this football ground; he and Tony had explored it once when they'd come here for a match.

A cellar where they stored all manner of lost things. Items that no one had claimed were stored down in that cellar and forgotten.

Ross ran for the stairs. He headed down to the cellar. It was dark down here, dark and sinister. There was only one entrance, only one exit. Once he was down here, there was no other way out. Ross stopped for a second to think. What if the shirt had the power to trap him down here?

He imagined the cellar door slamming shut, locking him in, just as he had locked the shirt in the box. He could be down here forever. No one knew where he was. He'd told no one where he was going.

At the bottom of the cellar steps he stopped. He looked up, half expecting that door to close, but nothing happened. He'd a feeling he knew why. The shirt had no power once it was trapped in the box, like that genie in a lamp from the old story of Aladdin. Someone had to open the box and let it out before it could work its evil magic. Ross was going to make sure no one would ever open that box again.

He ran to the far corner of the cellar and began pulling
back boxes and bags. They were all covered with dust
because they'd been down here for so long. He hauled
everything aside until the floor was clear, and there in
the corner of that cellar he pushed the box as far into a dark
recess as he possibly could. Even if they ever cleared this
cellar, they wouldn't see it. Ross was sure of it. Then he put
every box and every bag and every package he could find
on top of it.

At last he sat back. It was done.

He saw a movement in the dark cellar and for a moment he was afraid. He looked up. It was Tully, there in the far corner, watching him. He wasn't afraid of Tully now. Ross knew that he meant him no harm. He'd never meant him any harm. Ross smiled across at him, and raised his hand. Tully waved back. He seemed to be moving further into the shadows. Any moment now, Ross knew he'd be gone forever, swallowed by the darkness.

"We did it, Tully," Ross called out to him. "We put it back."

And Tully smiled at him, and disappeared.

Ross's emotions

All he thought about that day was the football shirt. He couldn't get it out of his mind.

desire

You can't steal from a dead person.

greed

What she said bothered him. Who else would think that he'd stolen the shirt?

paranoia

loneliness

Ross couldn't tell anyone.

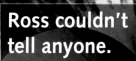

He bit into his knuckles to stop from screaming.

fear

Ross had to do something. He had to put the shirt back.

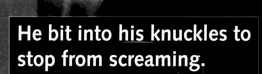

desperation

Ideas for reading

Written by Clare Dowdall BA(Ed), MA(Ed)
Lecturer and Primary Literacy Consultant

Learning objectives: understand underlying themes, causes and points of view; understand how writers use different structures to create coherence and impact; use a range of oral techniques to present engaging narratives; improvise using a range of drama strategies and conventions to explore themes; use the techniques of dialogic talk to explore ideas, topics or issues; set own challenges to extend achievement and experience in writing

Curriculum links: Citizenship: Respect for property; ICT: Multimedia presentation

Interest words: limited edition, suspicious, embarrassed, smirking, guilty, imagination, uneasy, unbelievable, somersaulted, genie

Resources: digital camera or video camera, ICT, whiteboard, paper, pens

Getting started

This book can be read over two or more reading sessions.

- Ask children to read the title and blurb and discuss the image on the front cover. What do they think the flowers by the tree signify? Prompt children to share their own experiences of seeing flowers at the roadside and how they feel when they see them.

- Discuss what sort of book they think this will be and why, e.g. a scary story because of the ominous lighting on the cover.

Reading and responding

- Ask children to read to p5 silently. Discuss Ross's temptation to take the football shirt, and whether they have any personal examples of feeling tempted to do something they know is wrong.

- Challenge children in pairs to make notes on the strategies that the author is using up to p17 to create impact, e.g. the use of very short sentences and chapters, the use of repetition.

- Ask children to continue reading to the end, making note of key moments in the story.